KU-765-864

SIMON AND SCHUSTER

First published in Great Britain in 2013 by Simon and Schuster UK Ltd, 1st Floor, 222 Gray's Inn Road, London WC1X 8HB
A CBS Company

MEADOW FRESH

For
Malachy Doyle
– MR.

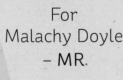

AQUAPHOBIC DRY SHAMPOO

ELBOW GREASE

To my
Grandparents
– KH

TUSK WHITENER

ANTIBACTERIAL HOOF WASH

curl tamer

Text copyright © 2013 Michelle Robinson

Illustrations copyright © 2013 Kate Hindley

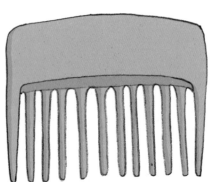

978-0-85707-579-6 (HB)
978-0-85707-580-2 (PB)
978-0-85707-899-5 (eBook)

Printed in China
10 9 8 7 6 5 4 3 2 1

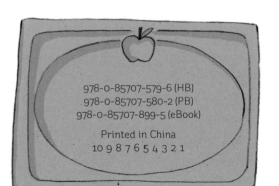

The right of Michelle Robinson and Kate Hindley to be identified as the author and illustrator of this work has been asserted by them in accordance with the Copyright, Designs and Patents Act, 1988. All rights reserved, including the right of reproduction in whole or in part in any form. A CIP catalogue record for this book is available from the British Library upon request.

HOW to wash a WOOLLY mammoth

Windsor and Maidenhead

38067100566128

HOW to wash a WOOLLY mammoth

MICHELLE ROBINSON · KATE HINDLEY

SIMON AND SCHUSTER
London New York Sydney Toronto New Delhi

Does your woolly mammoth need a wash?
It's not a very easy thing to do . . .

Woolly mammoths are quite BIG
and wool is notoriously tricky to clean.
Don't worry, just follow this step-by-step guide.

STEP ONE:

Fill the bath tub.

Fig. 1: Empty   Fig. 2: Full

If your mammoth is feeling thirsty, this may take a while.

STEP TWO:

Add bubbles.

STEP THREE:
Add mammoth.

Fig. 1: Broom

Fig. 2: Spooky mask

Fig. 3: Skateboard

Fig. 4: Heavy-duty crane

When all else fails,
there is always cake.

STEP FOUR:
Start scrubbing!
Don't forget to wash
behind those ears . . .

STEP FIVE:
Wash his big, fat tummy.

CAREFUL -
a mammoth's tummy is terribly tickly!

STEP SIX:

Make a SPLASH!

STEP SEVEN:
Now for the really WOOLLY bit.

You're going to need some shampoo - not too much!

Fig. 1:
Bubble bliss

Fig. 2:
Who me?

Fig. 3:
Hair-raising

Fig. 4:
Mammoth mullet

Fig. 5:
And that is?

Fig. 6:
Twirly-whirly

Fig. 7:
The King

Fig. 8:
Comb-over

Be CAREFUL
not to get any in
the mammoth's . . .

That's torn it!

STEP EIGHT:

To get a wet woolly mammoth down

from a tree, you'll need . . . .

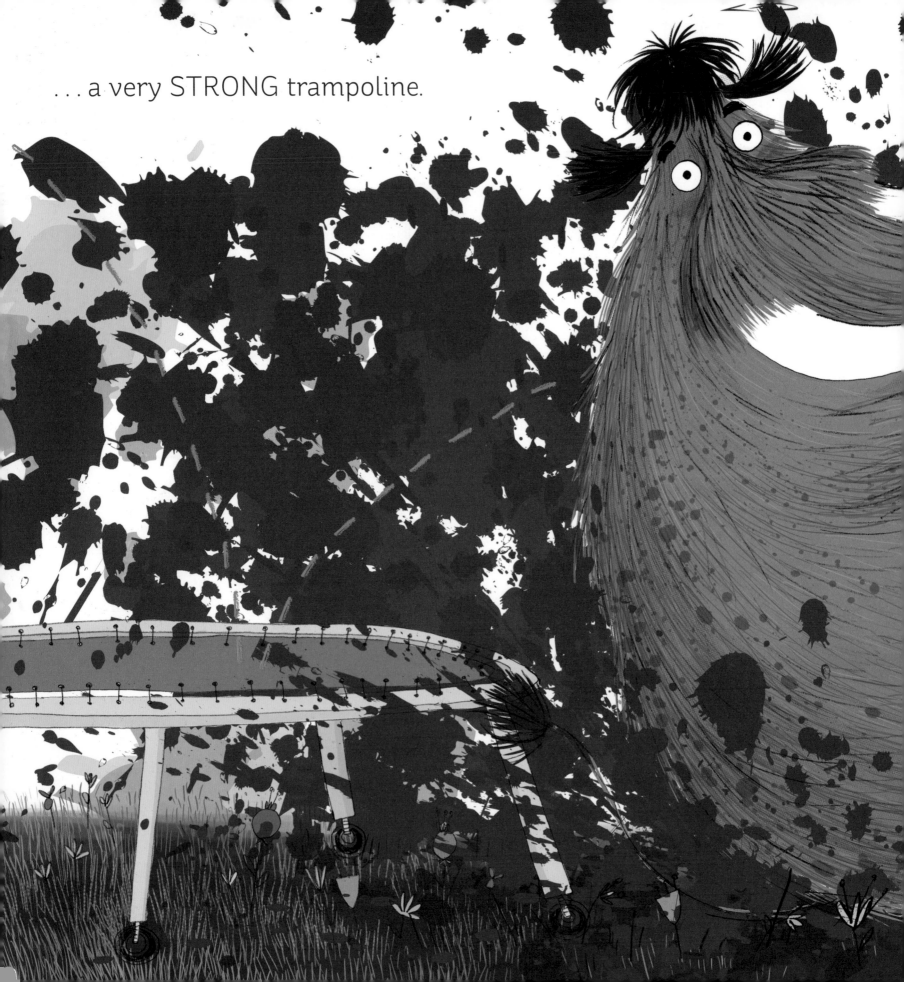

...a very STRONG trampoline.

STEP NINE:

Let him share a bath with YOU!

STEP TEN:

Throw in the towel

and SNUGGLE.